Secret Kingdom

From: Jackie

to: Victoria

D1113199

ORCHARD BOOKS

First published in Great Britain in 2012 by Orchard Books
This edition published in 2016 by The Watts Publishing Group

19

A CIP catalogue record for this book is available from the British Library.

ISBN 978 1 40832 364 9

Printed in Great Britain by Clays Ltd, St Ives plc

The paper and board used in this book are made from wood from responsible sources

Orchard Books
An imprint of Hachette Children's Group
Part of The Watts Publishing Group Limited
Carmelite House, 50 Victoria Embankment, London EC4Y 0DZ

An Hachette UK Company
www.hachette.co.uk
www.hachettechildrens.co.uk

Series created by Hothouse Fiction
www.hothousefiction.com

Enchanted Palace

ROSIE BANKS

ORCHARD

Contents

A Mysterious Find

"I think I'm finished now, Miss. Where would you like this box to go?" Summer Hammond asked as she packed up the last two books from her stall.

"I'm finished here, too," Jasmine Smith added, putting the last things into a box.

Mrs Benson smiled. "Goodness! That was fast work, girls. Well done."

Ellie Macdonald poked her head up from behind a table, tucking a wiry red curl behind her ear. "Hey, nobody told me it was a race!" Laughter danced in her green eyes as she stood up.

Jasmine winked at Summer. "It looks like we're the champions!"

"You're all champions," Mrs Benson said as she smiled at the three girls. "This was the school's most successful jumble sale ever, and it was all thanks to you!"

Although they were all very different from one another, Ellie, Summer and Jasmine were as close as sisters. They all

lived in the same village and had been
best friends since they first started primary
school. Summer was shy, and tugged
at her blonde pigtails whenever she felt
nervous. She often had her head buried in
a book, either reading about the natural
world or writing poems and stories
about her animal friends.

Jasmine was outgoing and always in a
hurry, with her long dark hair whipping
around her as she raced from one thing to
another. She loved singing and dancing
and being in the spotlight. Ellie was a
joker, and was always the first to laugh
at her own clumsiness. She was also very
artistic and loved drawing. Together they
made quite a team!

"It was nothing really," Summer said,
blushing at their teacher's praise. "The

books I sold were mostly my old ones from our attic."

"Well, they were very popular," said Mrs Benson. "And Jasmine, you played that guitar wonderfully. After everyone heard you, we sold it in no time."

Jasmine grinned. "No problem, Miss. You know I love music!"

"And the fashion stall was a great success, too – especially those superb Ellie Macdonald designs!" Mrs Benson picked up a T-shirt with a bold green and purple pattern on it. She looked over at Ellie. "Thanks so much for making one for me."

"Do you like the design I did for it, Miss?" Ellie said. "Green and purple are my favourite colours."

"You don't say!" Jasmine's hazel eyes

twinkled with amusement as she looked
at her friend's flowery purple and green
dress, her green leggings and her
purple ballet pumps!

Ellie chuckled, then
turned to pick
up her bag. But
as she did, she
tripped over
something
and fell to the
floor with a
thump.

"Ouch!"

"Are you okay?"
asked Mrs Benson.

"I'm fine – it's just my two left feet, as
usual!" Ellie said as she stood up. "But
what's this?"

She picked up the object she'd tripped over – an old wooden box. It was as large as her outstretched hand and made out of solid wood with a curved lid. The whole thing was thick with dust, but under the grime Ellie could tell the box was beautiful. Its sides were carved with intricate patterns that she couldn't quite make out, and on the lid was a mirror, surrounded by six glass stones. Ellie wiped the lid with her sleeve and could just see her reflection. As she held it, light swirled in the stones. It looked almost…magical. "How strange," she murmured. "I'm sure it wasn't here a minute ago."

Jasmine took the box and tried to open it. "The lid's stuck down," she said. "It won't budge."

Mrs Benson glanced at her watch. "Well, wherever it came from, it's too late to sell it now. Why don't you girls take it home – you never know, you might find a way to open it."

"Ooh, yes please!" Summer breathed. "It's really pretty. We could use it to put jewellery in. Let's take it to my house and try to get it open. I live the closest!"

The girls waved goodbye to Mrs Benson and raced out of the school playground. They all lived in a small village called Honeyvale, which was surrounded by hills and beautiful countryside. Summer's house was only a few minutes away from the school, just past the post office and

Mrs Mill's sweet shop. Mrs Mill waved as the girls flew by – she was used to seeing Summer, Ellie and Jasmine together!

When they arrived at her house Summer eagerly opened her front door and they pounded up the stairs, calling out a quick hello to Mrs Hammond before spilling into Summer's bedroom.

The walls were covered in wildlife posters, and books were stacked neatly on their shelves. Summer dropped down onto her white fluffy rug. Jasmine and Ellie joined her, placing the carved wooden box in front of them. Summer's cat Rosa came over and sniffed at it with interest.

"What do we do now?" Ellie asked

Jasmine grabbed a box of tissues from Summer's bedside table. "We clean it."

The three friends worked together,

wiping away the dust and dirt that
covered the box.

"Wow. It's absolutely gorgeous!"
exclaimed Summer. She traced her finger
over the side of the box. Now it was clean,
she could see that the sides were covered
in delicate carvings of fairies, unicorns
and other magical creatures. The glass

stones that studded the lid were a deep
green, and shone like emeralds.

"What do you think is inside?" Ellie
whispered.

Jasmine shrugged. "Let's have another
go at opening it."

Ellie passed Jasmine a ruler from
Summer's desk and they carefully tried to
prise the lid open, but it refused to budge.

Summer sighed. "There has to be a way
to open it." She rubbed at the mirrored
glass of the lid with her tissue to clean
away the last traces of dust, then gasped.
"The mirror. It's…glowing!"

"It is," squeaked Ellie, staring wide-eyed
at the box. "And look – there are words in
it!"

Jasmine frowned. With a shaky voice she
read out the words that had appeared:

"Ten digits make two,
Though two are too few.
But three lots of two,
On each jewel will do."

The three friends looked at one another in amazement.

"I-is it a trick?" Summer stammered.

"Or maybe magic?" Ellie whispered.

"I don't know," Jasmine said

thoughtfully. "But the words look like a riddle. My grandmother is always giving me Hindi riddles to solve. She says it's good for my brain."

"Do you think you can solve this one?" Ellie asked.

Jasmine stared at the words. "Well," she began, "Grandma says that riddles don't always mean what they seem to mean. You've got to look at things sideways. 'Ten digits make two'… Well, the word 'digits' normally means numbers, but it can also mean fingers, right?"

Summer and Ellie nodded.

Jasmine sat up a bit straighter. "So if ten digits refers to your fingers and thumbs, that would make two…"

"Hands!" Ellie finished. "Ten digits makes two hands! 'But two are too few', so two hands aren't enough!"

"'But three lots of two, on each jewel will do'," said Summer. "So three lots of two means three sets of hands."

Ellie's eyes gleamed. "That's it! The riddle is telling the three of us to put our hands on the green jewels!"

"What are we waiting for?" Jasmine said. "Let's do it!" She placed her hands on two of the glinting stones. Ellie and Summer hesitated for a moment but then lowered their palms to the jewels too.

Their hands completely covered the box.

It might just have been Jasmine and
Ellie's hands next to hers, but it seemed
to Summer that the box was growing
warmer underneath her touch. "Can
you feel that?" she whispered. Ellie and
Jasmine nodded, their eyes wide with
amazement.

Suddenly, the mirror glowed brightly
and light spilled out from between
their fingers. Gasping, the girls moved
their hands – and the box burst open!
A beam of glittering light streamed
out and bounced off the walls of
Summer's bedroom. The girls watched in
amazement as the beam hit her wardrobe,
and disappeared.

"Wow! Did you see that?" Ellie cried,
staring down at the box, which was shut

again as if nothing had happened. The others nodded. "I wonder if—"

Suddenly, she was interrupted by hangers clattering inside Summer's wardrobe.

"It's dark, so dark," wailed a deep voice.

"Please calm down, Your Majesty," a tinkly girl's voice replied. "I'll find a way out."

"Ouch!" cried the other voice. "Careful where you put your elbows, Trixibelle!"

Summer, Ellie and Jasmine stared at one another in astonishment.

"Does your wardrobe normally do that?" Ellie asked Summer.

"Um, no. M–m–maybe we should hide?" Summer looked pale.

Just then, the wardrobe door wobbled, and all three girls leapt to their feet.

"Ah, here it is. I think I've found a way out," the tinkly voice said.

Jasmine narrowed her eyes. She grabbed Summer's ruler and held it out in front of her like a sword.

"Who's there?" she shouted, bravely.

As if in answer, the wardrobe door sprang open and something small and colourful zoomed out into the air. Sparks flew everywhere as it whirled about the room. Then, silently and delicately, a tiny girl came to a stop above Summer's bedside table. A girl floating on a leaf!

Unexpected Visitors

The tiny person was hardly bigger than
Summer's pencil case, but she was the
most gorgeous creature that the girls had
ever seen. Her messy blonde hair peeked
out under a flower hat, which matched
her colourful dress, pretty bracelets, and
shiny ring. She had big, bright blue eyes,
cute pointy ears, and a dazzling smile.

"She can't be real," Jasmine murmured,
staring in wonder.

"Do you think she's a-a-a…" Summer could barely finish her sentence.

"A pixie?" The pretty creature smiled. "Yes! And of course I'm real," she said, doing a loop-the-loop on her leaf. "I'm Trixibelle – Trixi, for short – and I'm a royal pixie. And who are you?"

Ellie and Summer were too surprised to speak. There was an actual pixie in front of them! Finally, Jasmine, who was always the boldest, stepped forward and introduced herself.

"I'm Jasmine. And this is Ellie and Summer." She pointed at her friends.

"Summer, Jasmine and Ellie," Trixi repeated. Suddenly the large, shiny ring on her finger twinkled with magic. She tapped it and a burst of sparkles shot out, forming their names in glittery writing in the air. "What lovely names!"

The three friends gasped in delight as the sparkles floated down and landed on their skin like snowflakes.

"Trixi! Where have you gone?" a voice yelped from inside the wardrobe. There was a crash and a pile of clothes tumbled out of the door. A small, rosy-cheeked man, the same height as Jasmine, emerged from under the clothes. He was dressed in a purple velvet robe trimmed with white feathers, and he

wore half-moon spectacles perched on the
end of his nose. He had a pointy beard
and a gleaming crown sat at a jaunty
angle on his thick curly white hair.

Trixi gave a little curtsy. "May I present
King Merry, ruler of the Secret Kingdom,"
she said, zooming over to him on her leaf
and pulling a yellow sock off one of the
points of his crown.

The girls looked at one another, then
quickly curtsied as well.

"Pleased to meet you," Jasmine said in
her most polite voice. "But what are you
doing in Summer's bedroom?"

"And what on earth is the Secret
Kingdom?" Ellie added, finally finding her
voice.

The king adjusted his spectacles and
peered at them. But instead of answering

the girls' questions, he said, "Oh my. Are you humans? Trixi, what's going on?"

"I believe we are in the Other Realm, Sire," Trixi said, her face shining with excitement.

"Goodness me!" said King Merry. "No one from our kingdom has visited the Other Realm for a very long time." He stared at the girls. "You see, the Secret Kingdom and your world, which we call the 'Other Realm', exist side by side but our paths rarely cross. I don't know how we've come to be here."

Trixi gazed around the room and spotted the carved box on the rug. "Look! There's your Magic Box, Your Majesty. Its power must have brought us here."

"This box belongs to you?" Summer asked, looking confused.

"Yes, it does," the king said with a pleased smile.

"And what sort of Magic Box is it?" said Jasmine, looking at it.

"It's one of my inventions!" King Merry said, proudly. "I'm not exactly sure what it does yet, though." He sighed. "I invented it because I need something to show me a way to save my kingdom from Queen Malice's meanness. The next thing I knew, the box had disappeared, and we were in your wardrobe!"

"Wait a minute," Ellie said. "Who's Queen Malice?"

"She's my sister." King Merry took off his crown and anxiously rubbed at his forehead. "You see, my home is a place of great beauty. A place where unicorns graze in emerald fields and mermaids live in aquamarine seas. But my sister, Malice, can't bear to see that beauty. She wants to make everything as dull and dreary as she is, and take all happiness from the land." King Merry stopped, his eyes welling up.

Trixi quickly tapped her ring and a white hanky appeared. King Merry blew his nose noisily before continuing.

"Ever since the people of the Secret Kingdom chose me as their ruler instead of her, she has tried to get revenge on us all by using her magic to make everyone miserable."

Trixi folded her arms angrily. "And now, on King Merry's thousandth birthday, Queen Malice has done the worst thing ever! She's used her mean magic to make six horrible thunderbolts and fired them all into the kingdom. Each one carries a powerful spell designed to cause a terrible problem. But we don't know where they've landed or what trouble they will cause."

The king picked up the Magic Box and examined it closely. "I hoped this box could help me, but instead I've ended up in the Other Realm! It's baffling." He held the box out towards the girls. "You might as well keep it. It can't help me if its magic has gone all wonky."

Summer, Jasmine and Ellie all leaned over to look at the box. Almost instantly a ripple of light spread across the box's lid, and another riddle appeared in the mirror! Ellie read it aloud:

"Look no further than your nose,
Look no further than your toes!
When you gaze at me you'll see,
The answer's clear as one, two, three!"

King Merry stamped his foot. "See! The box is all wonky! It's total nonsense!"

"It's a riddle, Your Majesty," Jasmine explained. "We've already solved one of them. I think we should try and solve this one – it could be a clue."

King Merry frowned. "All right. Well, as I invented the box I suppose I should have a go."

Jasmine nodded.

"Hmm…no further than your nose… no further than your toes…" the king murmured.

The girls watched doubtfully as he crossed his eyes to look at his nose, then leant forward to peer at his feet.

"Whoops!" The king's arms began to whirl like windmills as he tried to keep his balance. He fell onto the rug with a

bump. "I told you it was nonsense," King
Merry said sulkily, crossing his arms.

Jasmine, Summer and Ellie looked down
at the mysterious box again.

"'When you gaze at me you'll see, the
answer's clear as one, two, three…'" Ellie
said. "That's it!"

"What's it?" asked King Merry, looking
confused.

"I think the Magic Box is saying that
the three of us can help you!" Ellie cried,
pointing at the mirror's reflection of
herself and her friends.

"Of course!" Trixi clapped her hands
in delight. "The king's inventions never
normally work this well!" she whispered in
Ellie's ear.

"What was that, Trixi?" asked King
Merry, raising his eyebrows.

Trixi tried to look innocent. "Nothing, Sire. I was just saying that your inventions always work in the end."

The king considered Trixi's words and then smiled. "Yes, yes, indeed they do!"

Then he peered at the girls over his spectacles. "The Secret Kingdom is in terrible trouble. Queen Malice will stop at nothing to spread unhappiness. I rather

think that you three girls may be our
only hope! Will you help us?"
Ellie glanced eagerly at both of her
friends. "We'll do anything we can!"

The Place You Love Most

"You try and stop us!" Jasmine cried.

Even Summer was excited, despite still being a bit uncertain. "Can we go now?" she asked. "I can't wait to meet all the magical creatures, and—"

She stopped as the mirror on the Magic Box started flashing again, and another riddle appeared. Summer read it out loud:

"The thunderbolt is hidden close,
In the place the king loves most.
Magic made to stop the fun,
Must be found before day's done..."

Trixi frowned. "Well, King Merry loves the Secret Kingdom more than anywhere else, but it's so big. We'll never find the thunderbolt."

"I think the riddle must mean somewhere special," Jasmine said slowly. "Where's your favourite place in the Secret Kingdom, King Merry?"

"Oh, that's easy," the king replied. "It's the Wandering Waterfalls." He scratched his head. "Um, hang on...I do love the Topaz Downs. And the Mystic Meadows are wonderful during a pixie toadstool fight." The king shook his head. "Oh dear,

I can't decide," he wailed. "There are so many places I love in the Secret Kingdom. I wish I was back in my palace, on my special snuggly throne. I always think best there."

"Maybe that's because you're happiest there," Ellie said, her eyes lighting up. "Perhaps your palace is the place you love most."

"Why, I think you're right!" the king exclaimed happily.

Trixi bit her lip anxiously. "But King Merry's birthday party is being held at the palace today! If the first thunderbolt is hidden there, Queen Malice's spell will ruin everything! We must leave for the Secret Kingdom straight away."

Jasmine felt a buzz of excitement go through her. "How are we going to get there? Are we going to use magic?"

"Hang on, we can't just leave," Summer said, suddenly thinking of her mum and brothers who were downstairs. "What do we tell our parents?"

"Don't worry," said Trixi. "My magic combined with the power of the Magic Box will easily transport you to the Secret Kingdom. And while the three of you are there, time will stand still in your world – nobody will even notice that you're gone."

Ellie's eyes sparkled. "Then what are we waiting for?"

She held out the Magic Box to Trixi, who tapped the lid with her ring and chanted:

"The evil queen has trouble planned.
Brave helpers fly to save our land!"

Trixi's words appeared on the mirrored lid and then soared towards the ceiling. Then the letters separated and descended like a cloud of sparkly butterflies. They began to whizz around the girls' heads until they formed a whirlwind.

"Place the Magic Box on the ground and hold one another's hands," Trixi called.

The whirlwind now filled the whole

room. Jasmine squeaked in delight as
she felt her feet leaving the ground. She
looked round and saw that Summer and
Ellie had also been picked up by the
magical storm. She squeezed their hands
encouragingly and her friends grinned

back. The king had his hands over his
eyes, and Trixi was hovering just above his
shoulder.

"Secret Kingdom, here we come!"
Jasmine cried.

Then, in a flash of light, they were gone!

The Secret Kingdom

With a gentle bump, Jasmine landed
on something soft, white and feathery.
"Wow!" she squealed. The girls were
each sitting on the back of a giant swan,
soaring through a bluebell-coloured sky.

King Merry was riding another swan,
which was bigger than the others, and
the tips of its wings sparkled with golden
feathers.

"Enjoying the ride?" Trixi asked Summer, as she zipped along on her leaf next to them.

Summer nodded enthusiastically. "Where did these swans come from?" she asked, staring at their snowy whiteness.

"They're King Merry's royal swans," Trixi replied. "They're taking us to his palace."

"They're so beautiful," Summer murmured, reaching out and stroking her swan's downy back.

"This is AMAZING!" Jasmine shouted, as her swan took the lead, soaring through the clouds. "It's so much better than the SkyRyde at Honeyvale Fair!"

"I'm not sure about that," Ellie wailed, her face pale as she clung on tightly to her swan. "At least the SkyRyde ends after three minutes."

"You're doing really well, Ellie," Summer called over encouragingly, knowing that her friend was afraid of heights. "But you should look if you can – it's so beautiful!"

Ellie peeked over her swan's broad
wing, and gasped. Beneath them was a
beautiful island, shaped like a crescent
moon, and set in an aquamarine sea. The
shore of the island glittered with golden
sand, and in the distance the girls could
see emerald green hills and fields filled
with little balls of light on golden stems.

"They must be *sun* flowers," Ellie said to herself, giggling. For a moment, she even forgot how high up they were!

As they descended through the fluffy white clouds, Jasmine felt her stomach flip-flop as she saw mermaids – real mermaids – sitting on shimmering rocks combing their silvery hair. She could even hear their voices singing a hauntingly beautiful song.

"Welcome to the Secret Kingdom," Trixi said with a grin.

As they swooped down over the island, a fluttering flock of dragonflies rose up to meet them. A medley of colours surrounded them and Summer giggled in delight as one delicately landed on her hair.

"It's the most gorgeous hairclip ever!" Ellie laughed as she admired the dragonfly's beautiful, colourful wings.

King Merry proudly pointed out areas of the kingdom as they passed: the fairy flying school at the Windy Weir, Magic Mountain filled with sparkling snow-covered slopes and ice slides, and Unicorn Valley with its race course and enormous magical tree.

"Wow! Is that your palace, King Merry?" Jasmine asked, pointing to a fairytale castle nestled between two hills. A deep sapphire-blue moat hugged the castle walls, and magic seemed to glitter on the coral-pink bricks of the palace, like hundreds and thousands on cherry icing. The golden spires of the four palace turrets were studded with rubies and shone in the bright sunlight.

King Merry nodded. "Home, sweet home."

The swans landed safely in front of the palace gates and Ellie slipped gratefully to the ground, followed by Summer and Jasmine.

Trixi flew over to them. "Did you enjoy that, girls?"

"The kingdom is beautiful," Ellie said. "But I'm very happy to be on the ground again!"

"You must be joking, Ellie," Jasmine exclaimed with a grin. "I thought it was the best thing ever. I can't wait to ride on a swan again!"

"And it's just the beginning!" King Merry boomed. "Follow me."

He led them over to the gates. The golden railings twisted upwards into the shape of a mighty oak. As the king pushed them open, the branches flowered with blossom and a fanfare sounded all around them.

"The king is here!" Trixi announced as they walked into the beautiful courtyard.

A group of friendly green elf butlers, dressed in long black coats and white gloves, all turned and bowed. Then they returned to hanging up strings of bunting in the trees.

As the three girls looked closely, they saw that hundreds of glowing fireflies were clinging to the strings to make little lights.

"Oh my," the king breathed. "How handsome the twinkle-twinkle bunting looks. Trixi, my suggestion for the streamers has worked a treat!"

"I never doubted that your idea would work, Sire," Trixi said. She hovered above Ellie's shoulder. "It just needed a bit of pixie magic to help it along," she added in a whisper.

Ellie giggled.

As the king led everyone further into the courtyard, they passed a huge fountain surrounded by a cloud of sweet-smelling bubbles.

"Hang on a minute," said Jasmine. "That's not water, is it?"

Trixi smiled. "No. It's lemonade!"

"A lemonade fountain!" Ellie cried, running back and forth, trying to catch one of the fragrant bubbles on her tongue. Summer and Jasmine laughed as they watched their friend.

Behind them came the clip-clop of hooves, and they turned to see a beautiful blue pony led by an elf butler, and pulling a wagon loaded with brightly wrapped parcels.

"My birthday presents!" King Merry exclaimed excitedly.

But Summer wasn't interested in the gifts. She couldn't take her eyes off the pony and its aquamarine mane.

"He's gorgeous," she smiled.

"And he looks really friendly," Ellie added, staring into the pony's warm brown eyes.

Smiling, Trixi tapped her pixie ring and a rosy-red apple appeared in each of the girls' palms. But just as they started feeding them to the pony, Jasmine felt a chill suddenly crawl up her neck. A dark shadow fell over the courtyard.

"Oh, no!" cried King Merry. He pointed to the sky.

Floating over the palace was an enormous thundercloud. On top of the ugly grey cloud the girls could see a tall, thin woman with a spiky silver crown and a mess of frizzy black hair.

"Oh, no," Trixi whispered. "Queen Malice is here!"

Party Games

Jasmine, Ellie and Summer stared up
at Queen Malice on her cloud, their
hearts beating fast. Lightning crackled
all around, giving the girls the shivers.
Thunder rumbled loudly as the cloud
stopped above King Merry's palace just
long enough for a burst of rain to pour
right onto his presents.

"Your birthday party is ruined, brother!" Queen Malice shouted at King Merry. "Just you wait and see!"

"What do you think she did?" Summer asked the others. But neither Ellie nor Jasmine could guess.

Queen Malice gave a cackle of mocking laughter then the grey cloud sped off.

Suddenly the presents in the wagon began to shake and rustle. There was the sound of tearing as little legs pushed through the wrapping paper. Then the gifts leapt from the cart and started running away!

"My presents!" King Merry wailed.

Trixi tapped her ring. Although a stream of purple glitter flowed from it, nothing happened to the gifts. "My pixie

magic isn't strong enough to undo Queen
Malice's spells!" she cried.

Without thinking, Ellie dived forward
and caught one of the escaping gifts.
As soon as she did, the legs disappeared
and the present sat innocently in her
hands.

"Quick," Jasmine said. "We've got to
catch the rest!"

Everyone leapt after the fleeing gifts. Jasmine and Summer managed to herd three into a corner and pick them up. One ran straight through the legs of a surprised-looking elf butler, and Ellie, who was following it, couldn't stop in time and knocked him over! King Merry caught one by jumping on it, and then looked sadly at the present, which was now squashed flat.

"At least I can fix that," Trixi told him, tapping her ring and repairing it magically.

Eventually all the presents had been caught and changed back to normal. The girls stacked them back on the wagon.

Trixi blew her hair out of her eyes. "I wish we could find a way to stop Queen Malice once and for all," she said fiercely.

"And her horrid helpers, the Storm Sprites. The queen has all kinds of mean tricks up her sleeves, and we never know where she'll turn up next."

"She is such a bully," said King Merry. "And she's determined to ruin my birthday. I just know that cursed thunderbolt of hers is hidden here somewhere, all ready to cause trouble." The king's eyes brimmed with tears. "This is going to be the worst party ever – my subjects are going to be miserable and they won't have any fun."

"Yes, they will," Ellie said, her eyes flashing. "Because we're going to find the thunderbolt and stop it from doing any harm!"

"That's right," Summer and Jasmine chorused in loud, firm voices.

"And I'll help too," Trixi said, floating up to the king's face and drying his tears away.

"Thank you, girls," said King Merry, but his voice was still shaky.

"Bobbins!" Trixi called to one of the elf butlers.

The elf rushed over and bowed deeply.

"King Merry needs a cup of hot
cocoa with extra marshmallows," Trixi
explained. "And then he needs to change
into his party clothes. His guests will be
arriving in two hours!"

Bobbins led the king away into the
palace.

"Right." Trixi dusted off her hands.
"Let's go and find that thunderbolt!
We should start in the palace gardens,
since that's where the guests will gather
later. Remember to keep an eye out for
trouble!"

She stood up on her leaf and sped
ahead, leading the girls out of the
courtyard and into a maze with twisting
and turning paths that seemed to change
every time they blinked. Summer, Ellie

and Jasmine looked down every path and under all the hedges, but there was no sign of the thunderbolt anywhere.

Trixi led them out of the maze and past a beautiful pond that had a rainbow leading down into its depths. Trixi explained that the rainbow was a magical slide that could take you anywhere in the Secret Kingdom you wanted to go.

Finally, the girls walked into a garden filled with trees made of candyfloss.

Bunting hung from the trees and a group of brownies were busy putting lots of cakes onto a long table.

"These ones look amazing," Ellie said, pointing to a cluster of pink-frosted cupcakes.

"They're fairy cakes," Trixi explained.

"Oh, we have those at home," Jasmine said, sounding a bit disappointed.

"Really?" Trixi said. "The magical kind? If you eat one, you'll be able to fly for five minutes!"

"Wow!" Jasmine exclaimed. "We definitely don't have fairy cakes like that! Can we try them?"

Trixi nodded. "Just one bite though, we don't want the magic lasting too long. We've got a thunderbolt to find!"

Jasmine grinned excitedly and offered

the cakes to her friends, but Ellie shook her head. "Flying like a fairy? No thanks, I'm happy to have my feet on the ground!"

Jasmine took a small bite of her cake. After a moment's hesitation, Summer did the same. Instantly, a pair of glittering wings sprang out on each of their backs.

Jasmine flapped her wings carefully, and then shot upwards. Summer was soon beside her and they zoomed through the air, going higher and higher. The wind whipped through their hair as they did loop-the-loops and whooped with excitement.

Trixi twirled in the air with them, and then came to land on Ellie's shoulder. "Don't go too high up," she called to Jasmine and Summer.

Just as Trixi spoke, Summer began to wobble. "Uh-oh, my wings are shrinking!" she cried out.

"Jasmine, look out!" Ellie shouted as her friend's wings disappeared.

"Don't worry, Ellie," Trixi said. She tapped her ring and Jasmine and Summer suddenly slowed and landed gently on the ground.

"Phew!" Jasmine said, then grinned. "That was so much fun!"

Trixi winked at the girls. "Flying with leaves is much safer," she giggled.

Summer chuckled, although her legs still felt wobbly. "I think you're right!"

At the other end of the table, Ellie

pointed to some heart-shaped biscuits. "Hey, what are these called?"

"Endless cookies," piped up a brownie. He only came up to Ellie's knee. He was covered in soft brown hair, and wore a funny green cap. "You can eat as many as you want and never get full. Would you like one?"

"Yes, please!" Ellie took one and popped it into her mouth. "Yum! It tastes like strawberries and chocolate and ice cream all rolled into one!"

Trixi and the girls continued to look around the palace grounds, searching for any sign of Queen Malice's thunderbolt or the problems it might be causing, but there was still no trace of it. Eventually they reached an orchard where party games were being set up.

They could see a large barrel where
seven dwarfs were practising bobbing for
golden apples. Nearby, two tiny pixie girls
were busy wrapping one of their friends
in glittery pink paper.

"What are they doing?" Summer asked.

"They're getting ready to play Pass the
Pixie, of course!" Trixi said. "It's a great
honour to be chosen as the pixie in the
parcel."

Ellie grinned as she spotted a cheeky-looking imp drawing a unicorn on a wall. When the picture was complete the unicorn stamped its hooves and nodded its regal head.

"Let me guess," she smiled. "Pin the Tail on the Unicorn?"

Trixi nodded. "We'll also have Musical Thrones and Blind Brownie's Bluff. Then, of course, there's Musical Statues, but I've made the gnomes promise to change the guests back to normal straight after the game is finished this time." Trixi shook her head. "It's really no fun being a statue for too long – I hate staying still!"

Ellie and Jasmine laughed, but Summer's forehead creased with worry. "What are we going to do? The party starts soon, and we still haven't found the thunderbolt."

"We just have to keep looking," Trixi said. "We know it has to be somewhere around the palace. Malice's nasty magic will reveal itself soon enough."

Suddenly, a wild loud burst of laughter whipped through the air.

"What was that?" Ellie asked urgently. "Is it Queen Malice?"

Trixi crinkled her little brow. "No, it didn't sound like her."

The wild laugh sounded again.

"It's coming from over there," Summer said, pointing to an iron gate with ivy curling over the top.

"That's the Outdoor Theatre, where the King's royal performers are putting on a show to begin the birthday celebrations," Trixi said, flying towards the arched entrance. "Come on, we need to find out what's happening!"

Ellie, Summer and Jasmine raced towards the archway and then stopped in horror. There, sticking in the ground

next to the entrance, was a jagged black
thunderbolt!

Malice's Nasty Surprise

As Ellie, Summer and Jasmine stared at Queen Malice's horrible thunderbolt, another loud laugh came out from the theatre.

"We have to find out what trouble the thunderbolt's caused," Ellie exclaimed.

"At least someone sounds happy…" Summer said, hopefully.

They stepped through the gates. Rows
of marble seats led down to a wide stage.
All around them, performers lay in heaps,
tears streaming from their eyes.

"We've got the – hee-hee – the g-g-
giggles," a leprechaun managed to squeak
between screeches of laughter. "A-a-and
we don't know why!" The little man held
his aching sides. "The sh-show – hee-
hee-hee – starts in half an hour and all of
our scenery has been covered with black
paint."

Trixi looked angry. "Queen Malice,"
she hissed. "She's trying to ruin the show."
She tapped her ring and chanted a spell:

"With this magic, hear my plea,
Stop laughing and act normally!"

A shower of purple glitter spread through the air and settled on the performers. But they still couldn't stop laughing.

"Malice's magic is much too powerful for me. We're going to have to cancel the performance." Trixi shook her head despairingly. "It was supposed to be the grand opening to the party. King Merry's palace is usually full of laughter – and Queen Malice has turned that into a bad thing. King Merry will be heartbroken."

"Wait," Jasmine said. "We can't let Queen Malice win. Maybe magic isn't the only way to stop her."

"What do you mean, Jasmine?" Summer asked.

"The four of us can put on the show ourselves," Jasmine announced.

Ellie nodded, a smile stretching across her face. "If you can get me some paint and brushes," she said, "I can easily paint some new scenery."

"And I can write you a song to perform, Jasmine," Summer offered.

Jasmine glanced over at the giggling performers. "I think we'll need a dance as well. I can make something up."

Trixi's face bloomed with happiness. "And I'll help you all in any way I can! First, paint and brushes!" Trixi tapped her ring and instantly several brushes and pots of bright colours appeared.

Ellie knelt down and gathered them up. "Perfect!" She hurried over to the stage, stepping over a giggling elf. There were six backdrops at the back of the stage. Ellie shook her head in disgust as she saw that they had all been covered with big splashes of black paint.

Ellie squeezed her eyes shut and tried to remember all the wonderful places she'd seen from the back of her swan. In no time at all she had painted a whole new scene showing the mermaids she had seen in the beautiful greenish-blue sea.

"One down, five to go," Ellie said to herself determinedly.

Meanwhile, Jasmine had started practising some tricky dance moves. Her face was serious as she concentrated on making the steps as polished as possible.

Summer chewed on a pencil as she tried to think of lyrics for a new song. She looked up at the sky, hoping that the words might jump into her head. Her eyes widened. Even though it was daytime and the sun was shining, she could also see shooting stars and the moon glowing brightly in the sky. She blinked as she saw a face appear in the white surface of the moon and wink down at her. Summer smiled and eagerly scribbled something down. She knew exactly what the song's chorus would be!

Trixi whizzed between the girls, helping out where she could. Finally, the scenery, dance, and song were all finished.

"We've sorted out the show, but what about the poor performers?" kind-hearted Summer asked. She nodded at the actors, stagehands and musicians, who were still lying on the ground giggling.

"At least they're happy!" Trixi smiled as an elf gave a squeal of laughter. "But we need to get them backstage – and quickly! The king's guests will be here soon." She tapped her ring and conjured up some floating stretchers, which carried off the giggling performers. Trixi and the girls quickly followed them.

From the wings of the stage, they watched as the guests took their seats. The audience let out a huge cheer as King Merry arrived, wearing his ceremonial robes, which were so long they almost tripped him up as he walked!

Trixi floated behind him, holding up the end of his robes like a wedding dress as he made his way to his seat, looking very excited.

Trixi tapped her ring and two spotlights burst into life. "It's show time!" she said.

Jasmine took a deep breath, and marched out onto the stage. She felt braver when she saw Ellie's beautiful backdrops, with their paintings of mermaids, glittering golden beaches and snow-capped mountains.

From the wings, Summer and Ellie

peered into the crowd. They had never seen an audience like it. To the right, there were two real-life unicorns. To the left, a group of fairies with bright shimmering wings whispered excitedly. In the front row were the youngest pixies, elves, dwarves and imps.

On the stage, Jasmine didn't have long to take it all in. She had to start the show.

"Thank you for coming here from all over the Secret Kingdom," Jasmine called out. "Welcome to the start of King Merry's birthday party!" She threw her arms wide, just as she'd seen performers do on TV. The audience cheered in approval. Whispers rippled through the crowd.

Trixi grinned at Summer and Ellie. "The crowd loves her! I don't think they've ever seen a human girl before."

"We have quite a show for you tonight,"
Jasmine continued. "But first I must tell
you about something that almost stopped
it from going ahead at all."

King Merry's face went pale, but
Jasmine caught his eye and winked
reassuringly. She swiftly explained how

Queen Malice's magic had given the
royal performers a bad case of the giggles,
and damaged the scenery.

"My friends Summer, Ellie, Trixi and I
have put together a new show for you!"
Jasmine said with a flourish. "We're not
going to let Queen Malice ruin the king's
birthday, are we?"

"NOOOOO!" the crowd roared.

"That's the spirit!" Jasmine said,
beaming at the crowd. "We have a very
special song for the king. But before I
start, I think I need some backing singers.
Summer and Ellie, will you come out and
join me?"

Summer felt her cheeks go warm. She
reached up quickly to twirl one of her
pigtails. "I can't perform in front of all
those people," she whispered.

"Yes, you can," Ellie urged. "Come on!"
She dragged Summer onto the stage
and Trixi conjured up microphones for
them both.

Jasmine grinned at her friends. "Trixi?
Hit it!"

Trixi tapped her ring, and all at once
the instruments floated up from the
sides of the stage and began to play a
cheerful melody. With one more burst of
glitter from Trixi's ring, another sparkly
microphone appeared in the air and
Jasmine caught it.

The three girls began to sing Summer's
song. It was all about the Secret Kingdom
and the places the king loved best. The
audience thought it was brilliant and
soon started singing along with the
chorus:

"The Secret Kingdom
is a magical place,
Even the moon has a smiley face.
The king's birthday will
be a day of fun,
Malice's meanness will be undone."

While the instruments kept playing,
Jasmine handed her microphone to Ellie
and began her
dance routine.
Her dark
hair
whipped
all around
her as she
skipped
across the
stage.

The crowd clapped wildly in approval.

Ellie gave Summer a big grin. "We've done it. We've stopped Queen Malice from ruining the party and—"

SPLAT!

Ellie was interrupted by something hitting the scenery.

She and Summer looked up. Six strange-looking creatures with spiky hair, bat-like wings and ugly faces had swooped down into the open-air theatre, riding on mini thunderclouds. Their eyes were shining with mischief and their mouths were twisted into angry scowls.

Jasmine hadn't noticed them yet because she was far too

busy dancing. But Summer could see that in their hands they held big fat raindrops, which they began hurling towards the stage!

"Trixi!" Summer hissed, beckoning to the pixie, who was hovering nearby. "Who are they?"

"Oh, no!" Trixi's face fell. "Those are Storm Sprites, Queen Malice's servants." The pixie looked worried. "And if we get hit by one of their misery drops, we'll be made as sad and mean as she is."

"We've got to stop them!" Ellie cried.

Summer nodded and looked over at Jasmine. A misery drop was whizzing straight towards her!

Ducking and Diving

"Jasmine!" shouted Summer. "Duck!"

Jasmine only just heard the warning
in time and dived to the ground as the
misery drop sailed over her head, missing
her by centimetres. Straightaway she
jumped back to her feet and tap-danced
on the spot, trying to keep the show
going.

"Those are Queen Malice's Storm Sprites!" Ellie called to her, pointing up at the sky toward where the creatures were hovering.

Trixi flew over to Jasmine. "We have to get off the stage. Getting hit by one of those misery drops would be really bad news."

Jasmine kept on tap-dancing. "We can't stop," she said. "We mustn't let them ruin everything!"

From the stage, Ellie and Summer saw King Merry fall out of his chair as he dodged one of the Storm Sprites' misery drops.

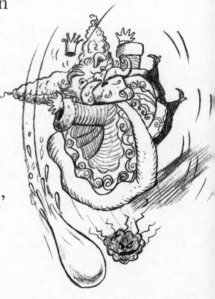

Drops were now splashing into the audience, causing little rain clouds to spring up over everyone's heads. Soon unicorns, pixies and elves were all looking miserable.

Up on the stage, Jasmine began to dance faster. "Hey, sprites!" she called. "Bet you can't get me!"

The six Storm Sprites narrowed their eyes and flew towards her.

"We're going to soak you!" one of the sprites said with a sneer. "Splish, splash, splosh!" He hurled a misery drop at Jasmine, but she jumped out of the way.

"Oi, careful!" another sprite screeched. "You almost got me." The two sprites began to argue.

"That's it!" Jasmine said to herself. "If we can get the sprites to throw the drops at one another, we can turn their magic back on them!"

"Jasmine, come on!" Summer called as she and Ellie dodged and dived to avoid the misery drops splattered around them. "Duck!"

But Jasmine stood absolutely still.

"Jasmine, what are you doing?" Ellie called.

"Quick, get beside me and wait for my shout," Jasmine said. To her left she could see three Storm Sprites whizzing towards her on their rain clouds, misery drops raised. Another three were coming at her from the right. Ellie and Summer raced over to stand next to her.

"They're going to splash us!" Ellie cried.

"One…two…three…DUCK!" Jasmine shouted.

All three girls dropped to the ground
just as all the sprites released their misery
drops. There was a great SPLAT, and then
a series of loud wails. All six sprites had
been hit, and each one was soaking wet!
Little storm clouds broke out over each
sprite's head.

"Ugh!" one sprite whined. "I'm all cold and wet! I've got water up my nose. Look, I can blow bubbles."

"Me too," said the sprite next to him, letting all his drops fall to the ground and sitting on his cloud gloomily.

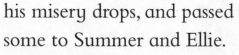

Jasmine rushed forward, scooped up his misery drops, and passed some to Summer and Ellie.

"Take that!" she yelled as they pelted the Storm Sprites with misery drops.

"Argh!" yelled a sprite. "This is horrible. Let's get out of here!"

The sprites' rain clouds rose into the air and zoomed quickly out of sight.

"Yes!" Jasmine cheered. "We did it!"

Ellie jumped up and down in delight.

But Summer was staring at the misery drop in her hands with a twinkle in her eye. "I have an idea," she whispered. "Maybe the misery drops can cure the performers' giggles."

"Let's ask Trixi," Jasmine suggested, waving her over.

The little pixie was helping King Merry, who had been hit with a misery drop and was sitting gloomily in a puddle with a cloud raining down on his head.

"He's so sad!" Trixi sighed as she flew over to the girls.

Summer quickly explained her plan and Trixi's eyes shone brightly. "Good idea, Summer!"

Summer held out the shining droplet

and Trixi pointed at it. Her pixie ring
gleamed as she chanted:

"Go to the performers, misery drop,
And make their silly laughing stop!"

The drop vanished, and there was a
loud cracking sound from outside the
theatre.

"What was that noise?" Summer asked,
pulling her two friends to their feet.

"I think I know," said Trixi. She darted
to the theatre gates, and reappeared with
a mass of ugly black splinters floating
behind her in a cloud of dust. "They're
from Queen Malice's thunderbolt," she
explained.

"Yuck!" Summer said, peering at the
splinters. "Even now, it still looks nasty.

But what happened to it?"

"When you girls helped the performers and stopped Queen Malice from ruining the show, it broke her spell," explained Trixi. "And the thunderbolt must have shattered."

Trixi tapped her ring and the splinters disappeared in a puff of smoke.

An angry shriek sounded, and suddenly a storm cloud appeared overhead with a familiar figure on top. It was Queen Malice, shaking her bony fist. "You human girls may have broken my first thunderbolt," she screeched, "but next time you won't be so lucky. My next one is hidden so well that you'll never find it!" She threw her head back and laughed as she zoomed away on her cloud.

Trixi shuddered.

"Don't worry, Trixi," Jasmine said fiercely. "We won't let her ruin the Secret Kingdom."

The others nodded.

"Oh, look," Summer smiled. "The performers – they've all stopped laughing."

Everyone turned to watch the royal performers walking out onto the stage. They were shaking their heads as if waking up from a bad dream.

In the audience, the rain clouds had disappeared from above King Merry

and the rest of the audience and they all
looked happy once again.

"Now that the thunderbolt is broken,
all of Queen Malice's mean magic is
undone!" Trixi said happily.

"Great," Jasmine said with a grin. "Now
that everyone's back, we can do a grand
finale to the show!" She turned to the
audience. "Sorry about the interruption,
everybody. I think we should all sing
along for this one. Are you ready?"

The crowd cheered. Jasmine whispered
something to Trixi, and the little pixie
tapped her ring. The instruments
immediately struck up a familiar tune,
and the whole audience sang "Happy
Birthday" to King Merry. His face broke
into a smile and tears of joy rolled down
his plump cheeks.

After the show had finished, King Merry came backstage to congratulate Summer, Jasmine and Ellie.

"If it wasn't for them, Sire, we would never have destroyed Queen Malice's thunderbolt," Trixi said.

The King smiled. "The Magic Box was very wise indeed when it took us to the girls. Summer, Jasmine and Ellie, will you continue to be friends to the Secret Kingdom, and help stop my sister from causing more trouble?"

"Definitely," said Jasmine.

"I can't wait to come back!" Ellie grinned.

"We'll be here any time you need us," added Summer.

The king nodded. "But you must promise to keep the Secret Kingdom a secret."

"We promise," Jasmine vowed. King Merry nodded at Trixi, and she grinned and tapped her pixie ring.

Suddenly, out of nowhere, three beautiful tiaras appeared in the air above the girls! Each one was surrounded by a sparkling glow. Summer's was a delicate rosy gold colour, with beautiful pink heart-shaped jewels. Ellie's had fancy swirls and a green diamond-shaped jewel in the centre. Jasmine's was a shimmering gold with intricate loops and pretty opals that seemed to sparkle with all the colours of the rainbow.

The girls gasped as the tiaras settled carefully on top of their heads. They fitted perfectly!

King Merry smiled. "These tiaras will appear whenever you are here, and they will show everyone that you are VIFs of the Secret Kingdom, on important royal business."

"VIFs?" Jasmine wondered out loud.

"Very Important Friends," Trixi whispered.

"Wow!" said Ellie, taking her tiara off to look at it. "This is the most beautiful thing I've ever seen!"

Jasmine and Summer smiled broadly as they looked at each other's tiaras. "Thank you so much, King Merry!"

Trixi smiled at the girls and did a little somersault of delight. "I'm so pleased that you will visit us again," she said. "I'll be here to guide you every step of the way. And this will help as well."

Trixi pointed her ring towards the beautiful pictures of the Secret Kingdom that Ellie had painted as backdrops for the show. As the girls watched, the pictures flew up into the air in a burst of twinkles. Then, as they floated down, the pictures joined together and grew smaller and smaller, then landed in Summer's hands.

"It's a map of the Secret Kingdom!" Summer exclaimed.

But as the girls looked at the map closely, they realised that it wasn't an ordinary map – it was moving! The sea around the island had blue waves that lapped against the shore. The trees of the forests swayed in a breeze, and the meadows of sunflowers gleamed.

"There are five more of Queen Malice's nasty thunderbolts somewhere in the kingdom, just waiting to cause trouble," Trixi continued. "The Magic Box will tell you when it has located one, and the map will help you find out where it is."

The girls nodded. "We'll be back whenever we're needed," Summer promised.

"Goodbye, girls," Trixi said, flying up to kiss each of them on the tip of her nose. "See you very soon!"

With a tap of her ring, Trixi conjured up a whirlwind that scooped the girls up into the air, higher and higher. Then, with a bright flash of light, they found themselves landing gently back in Summer's bedroom.

Jasmine stared down at the Magic Box, which was still sitting on the fluffy white rug, exactly where they had left it.

"Did all that just happen, or was I having a strange dream?" she said. She put her hand up to feel for her tiara, but it was gone.

"It really happened," Summer breathed. "Look!" She held up the map of the kingdom.

"Where should we keep it?" Ellie asked. "It'll have to be somewhere secret. You heard what King Merry said – nobody can know about the Secret Kingdom except us."

As she spoke, the mirror on the Magic Box glowed. Then, to the girls' amazement, the box slowly opened, revealing six little wooden compartments, all of different sizes! A shower of light sparkled from the centre of the box.

"It's the perfect place to store our gift!" Summer exclaimed.

Ellie gently placed the folded map into one of the spaces. It fitted perfectly! As soon as the map was in place, the lid on the box closed again.

"I wonder when the Magic Box will tell

us that it's time for our next adventure," said Jasmine.

"I hope it's soon," Summer said, crossing her fingers.

Ellie looked at the mirrored lid of the Magic Box and for a moment thought she saw King Merry's kind face beaming out at her.

"The Secret Kingdom needs us," she said softly. "I have a feeling we'll be back there very soon."

In the next Secret Kingdom
adventure, Ellie, Summer and
Jasmine visit

Unicorn Valley

Read on for a sneak peek...

A New
Adventure!

"There!" said Ellie Macdonald, standing
back to admire the pretty shapes laid out
on the baking tray.

It was a rainy Sunday afternoon and
her best friends Summer Hammond and
Jasmine Smith had come round to make
biscuits. Summer had designed hers in the
shape of hearts, while Jasmine had made

crowns. Artistic Ellie had created biscuit fairies with pretty wings.

"How long do we cook them for?" asked Summer, twirling one of her blonde pigtails thoughtfully. "I don't want them to burn!"

"Fifteen minutes," said Ellie, consulting the cookbook.

"Fifteen minutes!" wailed Jasmine dramatically, slumping down in her chair so that her glossy black hair flew around her face. "But I'm *starving*!"

"It'll go by in a flash," Ellie giggled. "I'll get the timer."

She jumped up from the table where they had been working, then stumbled as she caught her foot on the leg of her chair.

"Oops," she said, as it clattered to the

floor. Mrs Macdonald came in to see what the noise was.

"Don't you worry, girls," she said, admiring the biscuits. "I'll put these in to bake, and call you when they're done. I'm sure they'll be delicious, and you've made such lovely shapes! Crowns and hearts and even fairies. What imaginations you all have."

While Mrs Macdonald was putting the biscuits into the oven, the three friends exchanged a grin. Of course Ellie's mum thought they had good imaginations – she hadn't been to the Secret Kingdom, the magical land where only a few days ago the girls had actually met a real king wearing a real crown, seen fairies, and eaten magical heart-shaped endless cookies at King Merry's birthday party!

"Let's go upstairs while the biscuits are baking," suggested Jasmine. "And check on the Magic Box," she added quietly as the girls headed up to Ellie's room. "Just in case! You did bring it, didn't you, Summer?"

"Of course," Summer said with a smile.

Ellie's bedroom was long and light, with her art books and tools scattered across a big desk and the colourful pictures she'd painted pinned all over the lilac walls.

The girls settled down on the big window seat where Ellie did her painting. Summer carefully pulled the Magic Box out of her bag and passed it to Jasmine, who stared eagerly at its mirrored lid.

The box was just as beautiful as when they had first got it. Its wooden sides were delicately carved with images of magical creatures and its curved lid had a mirror surrounded by six glittering green stones.

"It was so lucky we found this at the school jumble sale," smiled Summer.

"We didn't find it – it found us!" Jasmine reminded her. "The Magic Box knew we were the only ones who could help the Secret Kingdom."

Read

Unicorn Valley

to find out what
happens next!

Secret Kingdom

Be in on the secret.
Collect them all!

Series 1

When Jasmine, Summer and Ellie discover the
magical land of the Secret Kingdom,
a whole world of adventure awaits!

Secret Kingdom

Bubble Volcano
ROSIE BANKS

Sugarsweet Bakery
ROSIE BANKS

Dream Dale
ROSIE BANKS

Lily Pad Lake
ROSIE BANKS

Midnight Maze
ROSIE BANKS

Fairytale Forest
ROSIE BANKS

Series 2

Wicked Queen Malice has cast a spell to turn King Merry into a toad! Can the girls find six magic ingredients to save him?

Secret Kingdom

Wildflower Wood

ROSIE BANKS

Swan Palace

ROSIE BANKS

Snow Bear Sanctuary

ROSIE BANKS

Phoenix Festival

ROSIE BANKS

Fancy Dress Party

ROSIE BANKS

Jewel Tavern

ROSIE BANKS

Series 3

When Queen Malice releases six fairytale baddies into the Secret Kingdom, it's up to the girls to find them!

Secret Kingdom

Look out for the next sparkling series

In Series 4,
meet the magical Animal Keepers of the
Secret Kingdom, who spread fun, friendship,
kindness and bravery throughout the land!

When wicked Queen Malice casts an evil spell
to reverse the Keepers' powers, it's up to Ellie,
Summer and Jasmine to find each animal's
magical charm and reunite them with their
Keeper – before their special values disappear
from the kingdom forever!

Available
February 2014

Trixi is ready for the magical Keepers' celebrations taking place in the Secret Kingdom! But can you spot the five differences between the two pictures of Trixi below?

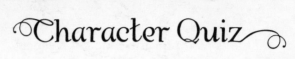

Character Quiz

Jasmine, Ellie and Summer are all heroes! But which one are you most like? Take our quiz to find out.

A baby bird has fallen out of its nest! Do you?

A – Take it home and look after it. You can't bear to see an animal in pain.
B – Climb back up the tree and put it in its nest.
C – Run for help – you really want to get the bird back to its nest, but you're not going up there!

Everyone's performing in a talent show! What would your talent be?

A – You couldn't possibly perform in front of people – you'll help backstage.
B – Singing and dancing – you want to be the star of the show!
C – Painting.

What's your favourite colour?

A - Sunshine yellow.
B - Hot pink.
C - Purple and green.

What's your favourite hobby?

A - Visiting the pet store to see all the cuddly animals.
B - Going to dance class.
C - Designing your own clothes.

Which personality traits best describe you?

A - Shy and quiet.
B - Outgoing and energetic.
C - Funny and clever.

Mostly A's

You are Summer!
You are kind and thoughtful,
and you love animals!
You're sometimes a little
bit quieter than your friends,
but you still love hanging
out with them and having
fun in the
Secret Kingdom.

Mostly B's

You are Jasmine! You are
brave and energetic. You
love being the centre of
attention, especially when
it comes to singing and
dancing.

Mostly C's

You are Ellie! You are
funny and clever, and you're
artistic too! Even though
you're scared of heights,
you're brave enough to do
things that scare you.

Secret Kingdom

A magical world of friendship and fun!

Join the Secret Kingdom Club at

www.secretkingdombooks.com

and enjoy games, sneak peeks and lots more!

You'll find great activities, competitions, stories
and games, plus a special newsletter for
Secret Kingdom friends!